Merry Christmas, SQUIRRELS!

Nancy Rose

Megan Tingley Books

LITTLE, BROWN AND COMPANY
NEW YORK · BOSTON

Most squirrels spend their winter
days hiding acorns in the snow.
Not Mr. Peanuts.
He is a most unusual squirrel.

Christmas is coming,
and it is Mr. Peanuts' favorite holiday.
He is full of Christmas spirit!

He checks his mailbox every day for Christmas cards. One day, Mr. Peanuts receives a letter from Cousin Squirrel!

Dear Mr. Peanuts,
Please come for a visit and spend the Christmas holidays with me. I promise it will be your best Christmas ever!
Sincerely,
Cousin Squirrel

Mr. Peanuts thinks a visit is a great idea. It will be fun to spend the holidays with his cousin. He gathers all his favorite Christmas sweaters. He has one for every day of his trip.

He starts to pack.
Who would've thought a
squirrel could have so many things?

Before he can go, Mr. Peanuts
has to make a path with his snowblower.
It is a little noisy for the other forest
creatures, but soon his driveway is clear.

Now he can hop into his convertible and drive to Cousin Squirrel's house. Don't forget to put the top up, Mr. Peanuts!

When Mr. Peanuts arrives, Cousin Squirrel is very happy to see him.

"This Christmas will be so much fun now that I have a friend to spend it with," says Cousin Squirrel. "Come inside."

Cousin Squirrel brews a
hazelnut latte for Mr. Peanuts.
"This is delicious!" says
Mr. Peanuts.

Cousin Squirrel wants to show Mr. Peanuts
that squirrels can have fun in the snow.
"What are these?" asks Mr. Peanuts.
"Snowshoes!" says Cousin Squirrel.

Later, they go sledding.
Mr. Peanuts zooms
down the hill.

Just look at that squirrel go!

The two squirrels build an igloo. "Now we have another hiding spot for our acorns," says Cousin Squirrel. (They are, after all, still squirrels.)

Cousin Squirrel builds a snowman.
Mr. Peanuts thinks the snowman
looks very fashionable indeed.

Next, Mr. Peanuts and Cousin
Squirrel build a gingerbread train.
It is the perfect size to ride in,
but Mr. Peanuts would rather eat it.
He never gets treats like this
at home!

"It is getting colder out here,"
says Mr. Peanuts.
"I know," Cousin Squirrel says.
"We should build a campfire!"

The open fire is warm and perfect for roasting chestnuts. Mr. Peanuts and Cousin Squirrel sing carols until the sun goes down. "Time to go home," says Cousin Squirrel. "It is Christmas Eve, and we have a very big day tomorrow!"

After wrapping presents, Mr. Peanuts and Cousin Squirrel sit in the warm living room by the fire and read together. Cousin Squirrel's favorite book is *'Twas the Nut Before Christmas*, but Mr. Peanuts prefers *The Nutcracker*. They try to wait for Santa to arrive, but before long they feel their eyes (and their whiskers) getting heavy....

When Mr. Peanuts and Cousin Squirrel wake up on Christmas morning, there are lots of presents under the tree!

Cousin Squirrel has a present from Mr. Peanuts.
He can't wait to see what is inside.

"Peanuts!" he says. "This is the best present a
squirrel could ask for!"

Mr. Peanuts has a gift from Cousin Squirrel, too!
What can it be? He opens it.

"You gave me peanuts, too!"
says Mr. Peanuts.
"This is just what I wanted."
MERRY CHRISTMAS, SQUIRRELS!

About This Book

Merry Christmas, Squirrels! and its companion title, *The Secret Life of Squirrels,* were inspired by the busy and inquisitive squirrels in Nancy Rose's backyard in Canada. When these squirrels became regular visitors to Nancy's bird feeders, she began taking photographs of them and eventually added miniature handmade sets for fun. She creates the sets, positions them on her deck, and watches through the glass door for the squirrels' approach. Her camera is on a tripod by the door so that she can capture the squirrels in action. She makes many of her own props, such as the mailbox, twig furniture, fireplace, snowblower, knitted items, and suitcase that appear in this book, and also uses some existing items, including dollhouse miniatures such as dishes, food, and toys, to decorate her sets. These days Nancy's friends, old and new, offer her little things to use in her sets, with some, like the ceramic stove, coming from as far away as Germany.

Amazingly, she does not manipulate the photographs digitally to position the squirrels in the scenes—she gets the squirrels to pose by hiding peanuts in and around the props. Nancy enjoys photographing squirrels in particular because she loves their curiosity. It's also challenging to photograph them—they move very quickly! Sometimes it can take more than a hundred shots to get just the right image!